Ha

Jacob (1785–   359)
Grimm are con........,   ; the
Brothers Grimm (*die Brüder Grimm*). They were
German academics and authors who specialised in
collecting and publishing folklore during the 19th
century. They popularised stories such as Rapunzel,
Snow White (*Sneewittchen*), Hansel and Gretel
(*Hänsel und Grethel*), and Rumpelstiltskin
(*Rumpelstilzchen*). Their first collection of folk tales,
"Children's and Household Tales" (*Kinder- und
Hausmärchen*), was published in 1812.

The rise of romanticism during the 19th century
revived interest in traditional folk stories, which
represented a pure form of national literature and
culture to the brothers. With the goal of researching a
scholarly treatise on folk tales, they established a
methodology for collecting and recording folk stories
that became the basis for folklore studies. Between
1812 and 1857, their collection was revised and
republished many times, growing from 86 stories to
more than 200.

The popularity of the Grimms' collected folk tales has
endured well, and the tales are available in more than
100 languages and have been adapted by many
filmmakers.

HANSEL AND GRETEL

The Original Brothers Grimm Fairytale

JACOB & WILHELM GRIMM

Brothers Grimm's
'Children's and Household Tales'
No. 15

FIRST EDITION
Translated by Rachel Louise Lawrence

Blackdown
PUBLICATIONS

This edition of the Brothers Grimm *"Hänsel und Gretel"* from *'Kinder- und Hausmärchen'* (First Edition, 1812; and Seventh Edition, 1857) first published in 2020 by Blackdown Publications

ISBN-13: 978-1657234604

Aarne-Thompson-Uther [ATU] Classification of Folk Tales
II. 300-749: Tales of Magic
    II.i. 300-399. Supernatural Tasks
        II.i.xxii. 327: The Children and the Ogre
            II.i.xxii.ii. A: The Children with the Witch
V. 1000-1199: Tales of the Stupid Ogre (Giant, Devil)
    V.iv. 1115-1144: Man Kills (Injures) Ogre
        V.iv.vi. 1121: The Ogre's Wife Burned in Her Own Oven

CONTENTS

Hansel and Gretel: First Edition

Hansel and Gretel: Final Edition

Hansel and Gretel

THE ORIGINAL BROTHERS GRIMM FAIRYTALE

HANSEL AND GRETEL
First Edition

Chapter One

The Bite of Poverty

On the edge of a large wood, there once lived a poor woodcutter who had hardly a bite to eat, and could barely provide daily bread for his wife and his two children, Hansel and Gretel. Ultimately, he could not manage even that anymore, and, in his misery, he did not know how to help himself or where to turn for help.

One night, as he tossed and turned in bed, worried about his plight, his wife said to him, "Listen to me, husband, early tomorrow morning, you must take the two children and give each a piece of bread. Then lead them out into the woods—to the middle, where it is thickest—and light a fire, then go away and leave them there, for we can no longer feed them."

"No, wife," said the man, "I cannot bring myself to lead my own dear children into the woods and abandon them to the wild animals, who would soon find them and tear them apart—my heart could not bear it."

"If you do not do so," said the woman, "then we will all die of hunger together;" and she did not let him rest until he said *yes*.

The two children were still awake, because of their hunger, and they had heard everything their mother had said to their father.

Gretel thought, *Now it is all over for me*, and she started to cry pitifully, but Hansel said, "Be hushed, Gretel. Do not grieve. I shall find a way to help us."

So saying, he got up, put on his little coat, opened the lower half of the door, and snuck outside.

The moon was shining brightly, and the white pebbles shimmered in front of the house like silver coins. Hansel bent down and filled his little coat pocket with them, as many as it could hold, and then went back into the house.

"Console yourself, Gretel," he said, "and just sleep quietly." And he went back to bed and fell asleep.

Early the next morning, before the sun had risen, their mother came and woke them both up: "Get up, children! We are going into the woods. Here, have a piece of bread each, but take care and save it for lunch."

Gretel tucked the bread under her apron, for Hansel's pocket was full of the white pebbles, and then they made their way into the woods.

After they had walked for a little while, Hansel stood still and looked back at the house, and this he did again and again, until his father said, "Hansel, why do you keep stopping and what are you looking back at? Pay attention, and keep marching on."

"Oh, father," said Hansel, "I am looking at my white kitten, who is sitting on the rooftop and wants to say goodbye to me."

"You fool," their mother said, "that is not your kitten. It is the morning sun shining on the chimney."

But Hansel had not been looking back at his kitten. Instead, he had been looking at the shiny pebbles he had dropped out of his pocket on the way through the woods.

When they came into the middle of the woods, their father said, "Now, children, go and gather some wood. I want to light a fire so that you do not get cold."

Hansel and Gretel gathered together some brushwood, a pile the size of a small mountain. They then set it alight, and when the flame burned high, their mother said, "Now, children, lie down beside the fire and sleep, while we go into the woods to cut down trees. Wait here until we come back and fetch you."

Hansel and Gretel sat by the fire, and when it was noon, they each ate their little pieces of bread until the evening. But their father and mother did not come back, and nobody returned to fetch them.

As it darkened and became night, Gretel began to cry, but Hansel said, "Just wait a little while, until the moon has risen."

And when the moon had risen, Hansel grasped Gretel by the hand and followed the white pebbles, which lay on the ground like newly-minted silver coins and shimmered and showed them the way.

They walked all night long, and as morning dawned, they came back to their father's house.

Their father rejoiced with all his heart when he saw his children again, for he had been reluctant to leave them alone in the woods. Their mother also pretended to be pleased by their return, but secretly she was angry.

Chapter Two
The Discovery in the Woods

Not long afterwards, there was once again no bread in the house, and one evening, Hansel and Gretel heard their mother say to their father, "The children found their way back once, and I let it go, but now there is nothing in the house save for a half a loaf of bread. Tomorrow, you have to take them deeper into the woods, so that they cannot find their way back home. Otherwise, there will be no hope for us."

The man's heart was heavy, and he thought, *It would be better if I shared the last bite with our children*; but since he had done it once, he could not say *no*.

Hansel and Gretel overheard their parent's conversation. Hansel got up, intending to pick up pebbles once again, but when he came to the door, he discovered that their parents had locked it.

Nevertheless, he comforted Gretel and said, "Just go to sleep, dear Gretel. The Good Lord will help us."

Early the next morning, they each received their little pieces of bread, even smaller than the last time.

On the way into the woods, Hansel crumbled the bread in his pocket, then stood still, as often as he could, and threw a crumb on the ground.

"What do you always stop, Hansel, and look around?" asked their father. "Keep to the path and keep walking."

"Oh! I am looking for my little dove," said Hansel. "It sits on the rooftop and wants to say goodbye to me."

"You fool," said the mother, "that is not your little dove. It is the morning sun shining on the chimney." Still, Hansel managed to crumble all of his bread and drop the crumbs on the way.

The mother led the children even deeper into the woods, to a place they had never been before in their lives. There, they were told once again to fall asleep by a large fire, and in the evening, their parents would come and fetch them.

When noon came, Gretel shared her bread with Hansel, because he had strewn all of his along the way.

Noon passed, and the evening went by, but no one came to fetch the poor children.

Hansel consoled his sister and said, "Just wait, Gretel, until when the moon rises, for then I shall be able to see the crumbs of bread that I have strewn, and they will show us the way back home."

The moon rose, but when Hansel looked for the breadcrumbs, they were gone—the many thousand birds in the woods had found them and gobbled them up.

Nevertheless, Hansel believed he could find his way home, and he dragged Gretel with him, but they soon lost their way in the great wilderness. They walked through the night and all the next day as well, until, exhausted, they fell fast asleep.

They walked for another day, but they were not able to find their way out of the woods, and they were so hungry, for they had eaten nothing but a few little berries they had found growing on the ground.

On the third day, they walked again until noon, when they came to a little house that was made entirely of bread, with a roof made of cake and windowpanes made of pure sugar.

"Here, let's sit down and eat our fill," said Hansel. "I shall eat from the roof, and Gretel, you eat from the window, which shall taste sweet."

Hansel had already eaten a good piece of the roof and Gretel had already eaten a few round windowpanes, and had just broken off a new one, when they heard a shrill voice cry out from within:

"Nibble, nibble, little louse!
Who is nibbling at my house?"

Hansel and Gretel were so terrified that they dropped what they were holding in their hands, and immediately after that, they saw a little woman, as old as the hills, sneaking out of the door.

She shook her head and said, "Oh, dear children, where have you come from? Come inside with me, and you shall be well." And she took them both by the hand and led them into her little house.

She served them a good meal of milk and pancakes with sugar, apple and nuts. She then made up two beautiful beds for them, and when Hansel and Gretel lay down in them, they thought, *It is like we are in heaven*.

The old woman, however, was a wicked witch who lay in wait for children, and had built her little bread-house to lure them to her. And if any children came under her control, she killed them, boiled them, and ate them—and that was a feast-day for her. So, she was quite happy that Hansel and Gretel had come to her.

E arly the next morning, before the children were awake, she got up and went to their beds, and when she saw the two of them resting so sweetly, she was overjoyed and thought, *They will be a tasty bite to eat for me.*

She grabbed Hansel and put him in a small stall, and when he woke up, he was surrounded by a wire mesh, locked up like a young chicken, and he could only take a few steps.

The witch then shook Gretel and shouted, "Get up, you lazybones! Fetch some water, then go to the kitchen and cook something nice. Your brother is locked in that stall there, and first, I want to fatten him up, then when he is fat, I am going to eat him. But for now, I want you to feed him."

Gretel was frightened and cried, but she had to do what the witch demanded.

Every day, the best food was cooked for Hansel so that he would become fat, while Gretel got nothing but crayfish shells. And every day, the old woman came and said, "Hansel, stick out your finger that I can feel if you are fat enough yet."

But Hansel always stuck out a little bone, and so she was surprised and bewildered that he was not gaining any weight.

Chapter Three
In the Clutches of a Witch

O ne evening, after four weeks had passed, the old woman said to Gretel, "Be quick, go and fetch some water. Whether your little brother is fat enough or not, tomorrow I am going to slaughter him and boil him. Meanwhile, I want to make the dough so that we can also bake it."

With a sad heart, Gretel went and fetched the water in which Hansel was to be boiled.

In the morning, Gretel had to get up early, light the fire, and hang up the kettle full of water.

"Now, be careful and watch it until it boils," the witch said. "I am going to light a fire in the oven and put the bread inside it."

Gretel stood in the kitchen and cried tears of blood, and thought, *It would have preferable to have been eaten by the wild animals in the woods, for then we would have died together and not now have to bear this heartache, and I would not be boiling the water that will be the death of my dear brother*; and then she prayed, "Dear God, help us poor children in our hour of need."

The old woman then shouted, "Gretel, come here to the oven straight away."

And when Gretel came, she said, "Look inside and see if the bread is already nice and brown and done. My eyes are weak, and I cannot see that far. And if you cannot see, then sit on the board, and I will push you inside. Then you can go around inside and take a look."

But once Gretel was inside, the witch intended to close the oven door, and bake Gretel in the hot oven, for she wanted to eat her as well. That was what the wicked witch was thinking, and that was why she had called Gretel.

But God allowed Gretel to perceive the old woman's intentions, and she said, "I do not know how to do it. Show me first. Sit on the board, and I shall push you inside."

And so the old woman sat down on the board, and since she was light, Gretel pushed her inside as far as she could, and then she quickly closed the door and bolted it with the iron bar.

The old woman then began to scream and wail in the hot oven, but Gretel ran away, and the witch miserably burned to death.

Meanwhile, Gretel ran to Hansel, opened the door to the stall for him, and Hansel jumped out. They kissed each other and were happy.

The whole house was full of precious stones and pearls, of which they filled their pockets. They then left with all haste and found their way home.

Their father rejoiced when he saw them again, for he had not passed a single happy day since his children had been gone, and now he became a rich man. Their mother, however, had died.

HANSEL AND GRETEL

Final Edition

Chapter One

In the Grips of a Famine

N ear the outskirts of a large forest, there once lived a poor woodcutter with his wife and two children—the boy was called Hansel and the girl was called Gretel. He had very little to live on, and once, when a great famine came to the land, he could no longer provide even their daily bread.

One evening, as he was tossing and turning in bed, full of cares and worries, he sighed and said to his wife, "What will become of us? How can we feed our poor children when we have nothing left for ourselves?"

"You know what, husband," replied the woman, "early tomorrow morning, we will take the children out into the forest, where it is thickest. There we will light a fire and give each a piece of bread, then we will go off to work and leave them by themselves. They will not be able to find their way back home, and we will be rid of them."

"No, wife," said the man, "that I will not do. How could I find it in my heart to leave my children alone in the forest? Wild animals would soon come and tear them to pieces."

"Oh, you fool," she said, "then all four of us will die of hunger, and you may as well go and plane the boards for our coffins;" and she did not let him rest until he agreed.

"But I do feel sorry for the poor children," added the man.

The two children, too, had not been able to fall asleep because of their hunger, and heard what their stepmother had said to their father.

Gretel wept bitter tears and said to Hansel, "Now it is all over for us."

"Hush, Gretel," said Hansel, "do not worry. I will find a way to help us."

And as soon as the adults had fallen asleep, Hansel got up, slipped on his little jacket, opened the back door, and crept outside.

The moon was shining brightly, and the white pebbles that lay in front of the house shone like silver coins. Hansel bent down and stuffed his pocket with as many pebbles as would fit.

He then went back inside the house and said to Gretel, "Be comforted, my dear little sister, and just fall asleep. God will not abandon us;" and he lay down in his bed again and slept well.

At daybreak, even before sunrise, the woman came and awoke the two children: "Get up, you lazybones! We are going into the forest to fetch wood." Then she gave each a piece of bread and said, "Here is something for your lunch, but do not eat it up before, for you will get nothing more."

Gretel tucked the bread under her apron, for Hansel had the pebbles in his pocket. After that, they all made their way into the forest together.

After they had walked for a while, Hansel stood still and looked back at the house, and this he did again and again, until his father said, "Hansel, why do keep staying behind and what are you looking at? Be careful, and do not lose your footing."

"Oh, father," said Hansel, "I am looking back at my white kitten, who is sitting on the rooftop and wants to say goodbye to me."

"You fool," the woman said, "that is not your kitten. It is the morning sun shining on the chimney."

But Hansel had not been looking back at his kitten. Instead, each time he stayed behind, he had been dropping a shiny pebble out of his pocket on to the path.

When they reached the middle of the forest, their father said, "Now, children, go and gather some wood. I want to light a fire so that you will not get cold."

Hansel and Gretel gathered up a small mountain of brushwood. The brushwood was then set alight, and when the flame burned high, the woman said, "Lie down beside the fire, children, and rest. We are going into the forest to cut down wood. When we have finished, we will come back and fetch you."

Hansel and Gretel sat down beside the fire, and when midday came, they each ate their little piece of bread. And because they heard the blows of the wooden axe, they thought their father was nearby.

But it was not a wooden axe they heard, it was a branch that he had tied to a dead tree, and that the wind was knocking back and forth. And when they had sat for a long time, their eyes closed with fatigue, and they fell fast asleep.

When they finally awakened, it was already pitch-dark. Gretel began to cry and said, "How are we supposed to get out of the forest?"

But Hansel comforted her, "Just wait a little while, until the moon has risen, and then we will find the way." And when the full moon had risen, Hansel took his little sister by the hand and followed the pebbles, which shone like newly-minted coins and showed them the path.

They walked all through the night, and as dawn was breaking, they came back to their father's house.

They knocked on the door, and when their stepmother opened it and saw that it was Hansel and Gretel, she said, "You naughty children, why have you slept in the forest for so long? We thought that you did not want to come back."

But their father rejoiced, for his heart and mind had not wanted to leave his children behind by themselves.

Chapter Two
The Discovery in the Forest

Not long afterwards, there was great scarcity again in every corner of the land, and the children heard their stepmother say to their father in bed one night, "Everything has been consumed once more. We have only a half a loaf of bread, after which the song comes to an end. The children have to go. We will have to take them deeper into the forest this time, so that they will not be able to find their way out again. Otherwise, there is no salvation for us."

The man's heart was heavy, and he thought, *It would be better if I shared the last bite with my children.* But his wife would not listen to anything he said, and she did nothing but scold and reproach him. Whoever says A must also say B, and because he had given in the first time, he had to do so the second time as well.

The children were still awake, and had overheard the conversation. When the adults were asleep, Hansel got up again, intending to go outside and pick up pebbles, as he had done the previous time, but their stepmother had locked the door, and Hansel could not get out. But he comforted his little sister and said, "Do not cry, Gretel, and just go to sleep peacefully, for God will help us."

Early the next morning, their stepmother came and got the children out of bed. They each received their piece of bread, which was even smaller than the time before.

On the way to the forest, Hansel crumbled the bread in his pocket, then often stood still and threw a crumb on the ground.

"Hansel, why are you always stopping and looking around?" asked their father. "Keep walking forward."

"I am looking for my little dove, who is sitting on the rooftop and wants to say goodbye to me," answered Hansel.

"Fool," said their stepmother, "that is not your dove. It is the morning sun shining on the chimney." Still, Hansel gradually threw all the crumbs on to the path.

The woman led the children deeper into the forest, where they had never been before in their lives. Once again a big fire was lit, and their stepmother said, "Just sit there, children, and if you grow tired, you can sleep a little. We are going into the forest to cut down wood, and in the evening, when we are finished, we will come back and fetch you."

When it was midday, Gretel shared her bread with Hansel, who had sprinkled his piece along the path. Then they fell asleep, and the evening passed, but nobody came to fetch the poor children.

They did not awaken until it was pitch-dark, and Hansel consoled his little sister and said, "Just wait, Gretel, until the moon comes up, and we will see the bread crumbs that I have strewn. They will show us the way home."

When the moon arose, they got up, but they found no crumbs, for they had been gobbled up by the thousands of birds that fly about in the forest and the fields.

Hansel said to Gretel, "We will find the way," but they did not find it.

They walked all night, and the next day, from morning to evening; however, they did not find their way out of the forest. They were dreadfully hungry, for they had nothing to eat but the few berries they found growing on the ground. And because they were so tired, their legs refused to carry them any longer, and so they lay down under a tree and fell fast asleep.

I t was now the third morning since they had left their father's house. They started walking again, but they only wandered deeper and deeper into the forest, and if help did not come soon, they would perish.

When it was midday, they saw a beautiful snow-white bird sitting on a branch, which sang so beautifully that they stopped and listened to it. And when its song was finished, it spread its wings and flew in front of them, and they followed it until they came to a cottage, on the roof of which the bird perched.

When they came near, they saw that the cottage was made of bread and roofed with cake, while the windowpanes were formed from pure sugar.

"Let us stop here," said Hansel, "and have a good meal. I will eat a piece of the roof, and Gretel, you eat from the windows, which will taste sweet."

Hansel reached up and broke a little off the roof to see how it tasted, while Gretel stood by the windowpanes and began to nibble at them.

Then a shrill voice called out from the room inside:

"Nibble, nibble, little louse!
Who is nibbling at my house?"

The children answered:

"The wind, the wind,
The heavenly child."

They continued eating, without a notion of being mistaken. Hansel, who liked the taste of the roof very much, tore off a large piece of it, while Gretel pushed out a whole pane from a round window, and sat down, the better to enjoy it.

Suddenly, the door opened and a woman, as old as the hills and leaning on a crutch, hobbled out. Hansel and Gretel were so terrified that they dropped what they were holding in their hands.

But the old woman shook her head and said, "Oh, dear children, who brought you here? Just come in and stay with me, you will not be harmed." She took both of them by the hand and led them into her cottage.

She then served them a good meal, of milk and pancakes with sugar, apples and nuts. Afterwards, she made up for them two beautiful little beds, covered in white, and when Hansel and Gretel lay down in them, they thought they were in heaven.

The old woman had only pretended to be

friendly, for she was in truth an evil witch who lay in wait for children, and had only built the little bread-cottage to lure them in. If any came into her power, she killed, boiled, and ate them—and that was a feast-day for her.

Now, witches have red eyes and cannot see far, but, like animals, they have a keen sense of smell, and know when humans draw near.

When Hansel and Gretel approached her cottage, she laughed maliciously and said scornfully, "I have them now. They will not get away from me again."

E arly the next morning, before the children had awakened, she got up, and when she saw them both resting so sweetly, with their full red cheeks, she muttered to herself, "They will be a tasty bite."

She then grabbed Hansel with her scrawny hand and carried him to a small stall and locked him in behind a wire-mesh door; he could scream as much as he wanted, but it was of no help to him.

Then she went to Gretel, shook her awake, and cried, "Get up, you lazybones! Fetch some water, and cook something good for your brother, who sits outside, locked in a stall, and needs to be fattened up. When he is fat, I will eat him."

Gretel started to cry bitterly, but it was all in vain, for she had to do what the wicked witch demanded of her.

Now, every day, poor Hansel was cooked the best food, while Gretel got nothing but crayfish shells. And every morning, the old woman crept up to the stall and shouted, "Hansel, stick out your finger, so that I can feel if you are getting fat."

But Hansel always stuck out a little bone, and the old woman—who had cloudy eyes and could not see it—thought it was Hansel's finger, and was surprised that he was not gaining any weight.

Chapter Three
In the Clutches of a Witch

Wwhen four weeks had passed and Hansel remained thin, the old woman became impatient, and would not wait any longer. "Hey, Gretel," she called to the girl, "be quick and fetch some water. Hansel may be fat or lean, it little matters, tomorrow I am going to slaughter him and cook him."

Oh, how his poor little sister sobbed as she was forced to carry the water, and how tears rolled down her cheeks! "Dear God, please help us," she exclaimed. "If only the wild animals in the forest had eaten us, then at least we would have died together."

"Just save your bawling," said the old woman. "Nothing will help you."

The next morning, Gretel had to get up early to hang up the kettle full of water and light the fire.

"We will finish baking first," said the old woman. "I have already heated the oven and kneaded the dough."

She pushed poor Gretel outside to the oven, from which the flames were already burning fiercely.

"Crawl in," said the witch, "and see if it is heated enough yet, so we can shove the bread inside." For when Gretel was inside it, she intended to close the oven and bake her in it, for she wanted to eat her as well.

But Gretel saw what the witch had in mind and said, "I do not know how to do it. How do I get in there?"

"Stupid goose," said the old woman, "the opening is big enough. See, I could go in myself," and she crawled towards it, and stuck her head into the oven.

Gretel then gave her a shove, which sent her far into it, closed the iron door, and bolted it shut. Whew!

Then the old woman started howling, it was quite horrible to hear; but Gretel ran away, and the godless witch miserably burned to death.

Gretel, meanwhile, ran straight to Hansel, opened the door to his stall, and cried, "Hansel, we are saved. The old witch is dead!"

Hansel then jumped out, like a bird out of the

cage when the door is opened. How happy they were! They threw their arms around each other's necks, jumped for joy, and kissed one another! And because they no longer needed to be afraid, they went into the witch's cottage, and there they found chests of pearls and precious stones in every corner.

"These are even better than pebbles," said Hansel, cramming whatever he wanted inside his pocket.

Gretel said, "I want to take something home with me, too," and she filled up her apron.

"But now, we must go," said Hansel, "and get well away from this witches' forest."

After they had been walking for a few hours, they came to a large body of water.

"We cannot get across it," said Hansel. "I do not see a bridge of any kind."

"There is no boat here, either," replied Gretel, "but there is a white duck swimming. If I ask it, it will help us across;" then she called out:

> "Little duck, little duck, can you see?
> Here wait Hansel and Gretel, on bended knee.
> There is not a bridge, nor boat in sight,
> Take us across upon your back so white."

The duckling swam up to them, and Hansel climbed onto its back, then asked his little sister to sit beside him.

"No," replied Gretel, "we would be too heavy for the duckling. It should take us across one after the other."

This the good creature did, and when they had landed safely on the other side, and walked on for a while, the forest became more and more familiar to them, until finally, they saw their father's house in the distance. They then began to run, rushed into the room, and threw their arms about their father's neck.

The man had not passed a happy hour since he left the children in the forest. The woman, however, had died.

Gretel shook out her apron, so that the pearls and precious gems scattered around in the room, while Hansel threw handfuls of them, one after the other, out of his pocket.

Now, all their worries came to an end, and they lived happily together.

My fairytale is over; see, there runs a mouse, whoever catches it may make a big fur cap out of it.

This title is now available as an audiobook!

About the Translator

Rachel Louise Lawrence is a British author who translates and adapts folk and fairy tales from original texts and puts them back into print, particularly the lesser-known British & Celtic variants.

Since writing her first story at the age of six, Rachel has never lost her love of writing and reading. A keen wildlife photographer and gardener, she is currently working on several writing projects.

Why not follow her?

 /Rachel.Louise.Lawrence

 @RLLawrenceBP

 /RLLawrenceBP

/RachelLouiseLawrence

Or visit her website:
www.rachellouiselawrence.com

Other Titles Available

Madame de Villeneuve's
THE STORY OF THE BEAUTY AND THE BEAST
The Original Classic French Fairytale

Story by Gabrielle-Suzanne Barbot de Villeneuve

Think you know the story of 'Beauty and the Beast'? Think again! This book contains the original tale by Madame de Villeneuve, first published in 1740, and although the classic elements of Beauty giving up her freedom to live with the Beast, during which time she begins to see beyond his grotesque appearance, are present, there is a wealth of rich back story to how the Prince became cursed and revelations about Beauty's parentage, which fail to appear in subsequent versions.

ISBN-13: 978-1502992970

CENDRILLON AND THE GLASS SLIPPER
The French 'Cinderella' Fairytale

Story by Charles Perrault

Her godmother, who was a fairy, said,
"You would like to go to the ball, is that not so?"

When her father remarries, his daughter is mistreated and labelled a Cindermaid by her two new stepsisters. However, when the King's son announces a ball, Cendrillon finds her life forever changed by the appearance of her Fairy Godmother, who just might be able to make all her dreams come true...

ISBN-13: 979-8696046723

ASCHENPUTTEL, THE LITTLE ASH GIRL
The Original Brothers Grimm 'Cinderella' Fairytale

Story by Jacob and Wilhelm Grimm
First Edition

"Go to the little tree on your mother's grave. Shake it and wish for beautiful clothes, but come back before midnight."

In the Brothers Grimm's version of a persecuted heroine's struggle to escape the hardships she experiences following her widowed father's marriage to a cruel woman with two beautiful but mean daughters, there are impossible tasks and helpful birds, a new name and an ash-dress, a Prince and three balls, a wish-tree and dresses of silver and gold.
Can Aschenputtel find happiness and a future full of promise, or will her family succeed in keeping her as their cinder maid?

ISBN-13: 979-8590909308

SNOW WHITE
The Original Brothers Grimm Fairytale

Story by Jacob and Wilhelm Grimm
First Edition

*"Mirror, mirror on the wall,
Who in this land is fairest of all?"*

The most famous of the Brothers Grimm fairy tales, *Snow White* is the story of a girl—as white as snow, as red as blood, and as black as ebony—who is the victim of a jealous Queen. But, with the help of seven dwarfs, she might just be able to live happily ever after...

ISBN-13: 978-1074705541

Printed in France by Amazon
Dictigny-sur-Orge, FR

10358000R00027